THE STORY OF
FLORENCE NIGHTINGALE

THE STORY OF FLORENCE NIGHTINGALE

by

AMY STEEDMAN

EVENTIDE

CONTENTS

CHAPTER I

DAWN

IT was in the year 1820, when spring was once more sowing the earth with flowers, that, on the 12th of May, a little English baby was born in the beautiful old city of Florence. The Villa Colombaia, where the baby first saw the light, was close to the Porta Romana, and outside the grim old city gate, the fields under the grey olive trees were bright with rainbow-coloured anemones and golden tulips, and the city itself was gay with flowers.

No wonder then that when the baby girl came to such a flowery corner of the earth, they should call her after her fair birthplace, the City of Flowers. The baptismal water was poured over her little fair head by Dr. Trevor, Prebendary of Chester, who gave her the name of Florence and signed her with the sign of the cross, "in token that hereafter she shall not be ashamed to confess the faith of Christ crucified, and manfully to fight under His banner against sin, the world and the devil; and to continue Christ's faithful soldier and servant unto her life's end."

The promise has been made for many a new little soldier enrolled under the King's banner, but seldom has it been fulfilled so royally as it was by that little maiden who was born under the blue Italian skies and who was to make the name of her birthplace shine in golden letters upon the roll of fame.

So it was that this baby started life with a beautiful Christian name added to the specially fitting surname of Nightingale. Her father had taken this name when he succeeded to the property of a great-uncle, so here was the small maiden surrounded at once with the magic of flowers and music, entwined in the call of her, and even a golden halo hovering around, for the word Nightingale in Italian is Filomena, and everyone knows that Santa Filomena is one of the best-loved and most honoured of saints.

Florence was not the only baby in the Villa Colombaia. She was, in fact, only the new baby. The little sister, who was now the old baby, could certainly not boast of any great age, for she had only been born the year before, when Mr. and Mrs. Nightingale were in Naples. She, too, had been called after her birthplace, the old Greek settlement of Parthenope, so had quite as dignified a name as Florence, but, indeed, neither of the children, as they grew up, were the least impressed by the dignity of their calling. Florence in a very short time became simply "Flo," and Parthenope became "Parthe" or even "Pop."

Mr. and Mrs. Nightingale and their two babies did not stay very long in Italy. The next year found them back again in England, preparing to make a home for themselves. The house of Lea Hall on Mr. Nightingale's estate was not quite suitable, so, while a new house was being built, they lived at Kynsham Court. By the time Florence was five years old, however, the new house, called Lea Hurst, was ready, and Mr. Nightingale had also bought an estate at Embley Park on the edge of the New Forest, so it was in these two beautiful homes that Florence and her sister spent the sunny days of their childhood.

Mr. Nightingale loved to have everything about him as beautiful as possible, and Lea Hurst was a specially charming home. The windows facing south looked over lawns and gardens and wooded slopes across the valley where the Derwentwater wound its way like a silver thread to the hills beyond, and on every side the view was lovely. But, surely, most charming of all must have been the sight of the two little maidens in their dainty muslin frocks, Leghorn hats and sandal shoes, as they played about the garden slopes, among the beds of purple pansies, blue forget-me-nots, and crimson wallflowers.

The children had each their special garden in which they worked diligently, planting, weeding, and watering, but it was Florence who was particularly fond of flowers. It seemed as if the City of Flowers had laid its charm upon her besides having given her its name.

The two little sisters were very fond of their dolls, too, although they showed their fondness in very different ways and brought up their families on quite different plans. Florence's dolls were all delicate and needed constant care. They spent most of their lives in bed, going through dangerous illnesses, while they were most carefully nursed by their little mother who doctored them and tempted their appetites with dainty dishes until they were well again. Parthe's dolls, on the contrary, were scarcely ever in bed at all. They led stirring lives of adventure, and when an accident happened and an arm was broken or a leg came off at the joint, it was Florence who tenderly "set" the arm and put the injured leg in splints.

And if it was interesting to nurse dolls, how much more worthwhile was it to take care of live animals! Florence looked upon all animals as her friends, more especially those who were unfortunate and rather ugly. Anything that needed her care appealed at once to her tender heart. It was she who welcomed and admired the very commonplace kittens which the stable cat hid from less friendly eyes. The old pony that was past work knew his little mistress loved him as well as ever, and that she always had an apple or a carrot hidden in her pocket for him. The birds, even the shyest of them, seemed to know and trust her. A pet pig and a donkey also came in for a share of her affection, and all dogs were her special friends.

Even in those early days, Florence was a very methodical little maiden, and kept a careful list of her collection of flowers with their names and the places where she had found them. But the earliest piece of her handwriting which has been preserved is a medical prescription written in a tiny book about the size of a postage stamp, neatly stitched together. A very childish hand must have traced the inscription, "16 grains for an old woman, 11 for a young woman, and 7 for a child."

It was the summer months which were spent at Lea Hurst, for in winter and early spring the family went to live in their other house, Embley Park, in Hampshire. There Florence and her sister were kept very strictly at lessons with their governess, for their father believed that girls should be taught quite as thoroughly as boys, and he planned his little daughters' lessons most carefully. With him, Florence learned Greek, Latin, and mathematics, and was extremely quick at learning all foreign languages.

The little girls were taught, too, by their mother to work their samplers and do fine sewing, so there was not much spare time in their days, but some hours were set aside for them to run about outside with their dogs and to ride their ponies over the Downs.

From her mother, too, Florence learned the pleasure of visiting the village people and getting to know them in their homes. She was always eager to be the messenger when there was a pudding or jelly to be carried to an invalid, or when there was a new baby to be inspected.

She was riding her pony over the Hampshire Downs one day, after she had been paying some visits with the vicar, when she noticed that old Roger, the shepherd, was having hard work to collect his sheep as there was no dog to help him.

"Where's your dog?" shouted the vicar.

"The boys have been throwing stones at him, your reverence, and have broken his leg," answered the old man.

"Do you mean Cap's leg is broken?" asked Florence anxiously. She knew the name of every dog about the place. "Can nothing be done for him? Where is he?"

"There's naught can be done, Missie," said the old man, shaking his head. "He's lying yonder in the shed, and I must bring along a rope and put an end to him this evening."

Florence turned beseeching eyes upon the Vicar.

THE DOG LAY QUITE STILL UNDER HER HAND

"Can't we go and see?" she asked.

The Vicar nodded, and they rode over to the shed where they found the poor dog as the shepherd had said. It tried feebly to wag its tail as Florence patted its head, and it seemed to understand that she was a real friend.

The Vicar, after a careful examination, declared that the leg was not broken, and that with careful nursing the dog might get well. Then Florence set to work to bathe the swollen leg and to follow all the Vicar's directions, and, in spite of the pain, the dog lay quite still under her hand, watching her all the time with his brown eyes full of grateful trust.

A message was sent home to explain where Florence was, and all that afternoon she watched by the side of the suffering dog and bathed its poor leg until the swelling began to go down. Then, when at last the shepherd came sadly in, carrying a rope in his hand, he found to his astonishment that Cap was able to stand up and give him a whine of welcome.

"You can throw away that rope," said Florence, "for he's going to get quite well now. Only you must nurse him carefully, and I will show you how to make hot compresses."

Perhaps, after all, Florence was very much like other little girls, for there are many who like to doctor their dolls and who are very kind to animals and who enjoy doing kindly things for the poor, but there was one thing about her which made her different to other children, and this special thing she felt from the time she was six years old.

Long ago, on the shores of the Lake of Galilee, some poor fishermen heard the Master's call, "Follow thou Me." Others, too, heard that voice, and with one accord they forsook all at the sound of the call. All down the ages that call sounded, singling out special people for a special work, and those to whom it has come have answered one by one. It was that call which echoed in the heart of the child, Florence Nightingale. Very faintly it sounded at first, and she scarcely knew what it meant, but deep in her heart she was sure that there was some special work for her to do, that she was called just as certainly as those fishermen of the Galilean Lake.

CHAPTER II

PREPARATION

ALL through her childhood Florence had this dim sense of a call echoing in her heart, and when she reached the age of seventeen the voice suddenly sounded more distinctly. She felt sure that God was calling her to His service. She had caught sight of the gleam, and she felt she must follow it now, although, as yet, she had no idea where it would lead her.

It was decided, at this time, that as Florence was seventeen and her sister eighteen, they should see something of the world and have various masters in France and Italy to finish their education. The home at Embley was to be improved and made larger, and meanwhile the family were to travel abroad for two years.

Then followed the gayest of gay times for the two sisters. There were balls and dances at Genoa, where the Grand Dukes were "exceedingly polite" to the fair English girls. In Florence they went to Court and found every one most agreeable and courteous. They attended so many operas that Florence became quite "music mad," as she described it. Besides all this, there were interesting places to be seen, strange people to be studied, and foreign politics to be considered, so there was really very little time for Florence to ponder over the old question of what work she was to do in the world. The desire to follow the gleam waned a little perhaps in those happy days when Florence first discovered that it was rather a pleasant thing to "shine in society."

It was so very easy for her to shine. She was tall and slender and very graceful, and if her face was not strictly beautiful, it was most interesting. Her grey eyes, which held rather a sad look in their depths, could yet flash into sparkling merriment, and she had the sunniest smile imaginable. Then, too, she was extremely clever and could talk brilliantly, so it was no wonder that she enjoyed the glamour of the gay life.

There were plenty of opportunities for the star to shine, both in Paris and when they returned to

London, where Florence made her curtsey to the little Queen Victoria. But although she enjoyed it for a time, the old desire to do something worth while seized her again, and she felt like a bird in a gilded cage, from which there was no escape. In her diary some time afterwards she wrote, "Life is not a green pasture and a still water, as our homes make it." She knew that to most people it was a struggle against terrible hardships, and she longed to be able to lift the heavy burden off their shoulders. "In London, at all events, if you open your eyes you cannot help seeing that life is not as it has been made for you," she writes. "You cannot get out of a carriage at a party without seeing what is in the faces making the lane on either side, and without feeling tempted to rush back and say, 'Those are my brothers and sisters.'"

She tried to do the best she could in her gilded cage, but the daily round, the common task, were by no means enough for her and she asked for a great deal more. What could she do? She knew, if she were free to choose, she would have no hesitation in deciding at once. She would be a nurse.

Now, in those days, it was considered really a dreadful thing for any young lady to even dream of becoming a nurse. Nurses were very different then. They were not at all unlike Sairey Gamp with her rusty black gown, rather the worse for a besprinkling of snuff, her want of cleanliness and her habit of drinking more than was good for her.

It was quite natural therefore that Mr and Mrs Nightingale were horrified at the idea of their daughter joining such a company. "It was as if I had wanted to be a kitchen-maid," said Florence afterwards, which really was putting it very mildly. She had made her plans quietly and had hoped to be allowed to go to Salisbury Hospital for a few months' training, but her family declared it would never do, and so all Florence's grand castles-in-the-air came tumbling down.

It was a little difficult for her mother and Parthe to understand Florence, and she was often a great puzzle and anxiety to them. She did not seem to care about the things that made most girls happy, and now that she was disappointed about the hospital work, her health began to suffer. It was a great relief, therefore, when her friends Mr and Mrs Bracebridge carried her off to Rome to spend a winter there with them. Florence hoped to get quite well and strong and ready for work, while her family secretly hoped that the change would make her forget the work altogether.

Certainly Florence had a royal time that winter and was too busy and happy and interested to worry about anything. The letters she wrote home told of all the delight she took in the wonderful sights of Rome. She could write most charming letters and she took the trouble to make them interesting. The day on which she first saw the Sistine Chapel she calls her "red Dominical, my golden letter" day — the most happy and glorious of all the days she had spent in Rome. As she gazed at those frescoes of Michael Angelo, she did not seem to be merely looking at pictures but to be gazing "straight into Heaven itself."

It was a great work which Michael Angelo had done — "giving form to the breath of God" — and perhaps it awoke to fresh life the longing to go for-

"YOU CANNOT GET OUT OF A CARRIAGE AT A PARTY WITHOUT MAKING THE LINE ON EITHER SIDE, SEEING WHAT IS IN THE FACES, AND WITHOUT FEELING TEMPTED TO RUSH BACK AND SAY, 'THOSE ARE MY BROTHERS AND SISTERS.'"

ward and do her own piece of work, to once more strive to "follow the gleam."

All the beauty of the wonderful city helped to make that a golden day in her life. She describes the look of the Campagna when "the long stripes of violet and pomegranate-coloured light swept over the plain like waves," when great crimson lights and shadows "like the carnation-coloured wings of angels, themselves invisible," came swooping along, and then, in the evening, the walk in the silvery moonlight over Ponte S. Angelo, when she breathed a little prayer to S. Michael to help her to be thankful for all this beauty. She belonged to the Anglican Church, but she was quick to see the beauty and helpfulness in other forms of religion, and after mentioning the prayer to S. Michael, she adds, "Why Protestants should shut themselves out in solitary pride from the Communion of Saints in Heaven and in earth, I never could understand."

She was not at all confused with all the wonderful things she saw in the Eternal City, although she says she often felt like a pagan in the morning, a Jew in the afternoon, and a Christian in the evening. All the time she was trying to learn something more about God, and that intense interest ran through all the beautiful sights like a thread through pearls.

There were exciting times, too, where the Tricolour of Italy was flown from the capital, where money and jewellery were poured onto the patriotic altars set up in the public squares, and a torchlight procession swept through the city, followed by singing crowds.

"I was certainly born to be a rag-tag and bob-tail," she writes, "for when I hear of a popular demonstration, I am nothing better than a ragamuffin."

But there was something in Rome which she found even more interesting than pictures and processions, and this was the work done by Sisters of Charity at a convent school. Their devotion to their work greatly impressed her, and she felt she had discovered the real secret of their success. It was a secret which she never forgot, and she always looked upon devotion as the great motive power in the work of nursing.

That winter at Rome was a time to be remembered for many reasons, and for one especially —

that it was there that her friendship began with Mr. and Mrs. Sidney Herbert, a friendship which was to help her so greatly in after years.

But if her mother had fondly hoped that foreign travel would make her daughter more content with home, she must have been grievously disappointed. Florence returned more restless than ever and more bent on finding work to do. She was eager to help with the Ragged School work in London, but when she suggested going to the slums to see for herself what help the poor needed, she was told that "a young woman in your station of life cannot go out in London without a servant." And so the struggle went on.

The years were slipping past and there seemed nothing to mark them. She went abroad again, to Egypt and Greece this time, but it all felt rather a weary waste of energy, although she was keen to learn everything she could and make it a time of preparation so that when the work came she might be ready for it. What she enjoyed most of all was a visit to Kaiserwerth, a place in Germany where deaconesses were trained to work in hospital and school. To this place she returned later a second time and stayed there for several months, living as one of the Sisters and learning all she could learn. It was very different to the kind of life she had lived at home, but she was as happy there as the day was long, in spite of poor food and hard work.

This visit to Kaiserwerth perhaps fixed her more firmly than ever in her purpose to become a Hospital Sister. "I had three paths among which to choose," she wrote in her diary. "I might have been a literary woman, or a married woman, or a Hospital Sister." She did not choose to be a literary woman because she cared more for deeds than words; she did not marry because she felt it would interfere with her work, and she was determined that the call should come first. She was thirty now — the time, she reminded herself, when the Master began His mission — and she felt that the hour had come when she ought to make a stand. She could not bear to grieve her home people, but she could wait no longer.

So, at last, a little freedom was granted to her, and it was arranged that she should spend half the year at home and half in doing what she wanted.

Her first plan was to go to Paris to study the work of the Sisters of Charity there, and after that it was arranged that she should take charge of a home for sick governesses and poor, friendless ladies in Harley Street.

Thus it was that Florence Nightingale's work was at last really begun, and not long after she had buckled on her armour and furnished her home, the great call to arms came, and she was ready to answer, "Here," and to step at once into the place which she alone could fill.

CHAPTER III

THE BURDEN AND HEAT OF THE DAY

THE Crimean War had begun, the glorious battle of Alma had been fought and won. There was mourning in many an English home for the men who had fallen, but the whole country rang with the praises of those brave soldiers, and England did not grudge the sacrifice. But by and by, news began to arrive which aroused public indignation. It was said that the wounded soldiers were dying from neglect, that their only nurses were old Chelsea pensioners, too aged and helpless to be of any use, that there was no proper food for them, not nearly enough doctors, and not even a proper supply of linen to make bandages. A letter to The Times from a special correspondent said that "the manner in which the sick and wounded are treated is worthy only of the Savages of Dahomey." The same letter spoke in high praise of what the French doctors were doing and of the usefulness of their Sisters of Charity who had come out to help and were excellent nurses. It surely behoved the English people to be up and doing for the English soldiers, to put an end to such a disgraceful state of things.

"Why have we no Sisters of Charity?" was the cry that echoed far and near. "Were there not women in England as ready and willing to nurse the wounded soldiers as there had been found in France?"

There was one Englishwoman, at least, who needed no urging. In a flash, Florence Nightingale realized that here was the opportunity she had been waiting for, the work for which she had been preparing herself all those long ten years.

Many people were eager and willing to help with money or service, but there was only one person who was fit and ready to undertake the work, and that was Florence Nightingale. She had had a hospital training, she was a splendid business woman and organizer, and she was ready to start at once. Her friend, Mr. Herbert, was now Secretary of War and helped her as no one else could have done. Through him, the Government asked her to accept the office of Superintendent of the female nursing establishment in the Military Hospitals in Turkey and gave her full authority to choose her own nurses, make her own rules and regulations, and take complete control of those under her. Whatever difficulties awaited her, she was promised every help from the home government, and letters were sent to Lord Raglan, the Commander-in-Chief, and those in authority in the hospitals to make her path as smooth as possible.

But even with all this promised help, who could foresee what a terrible time of difficulty, danger, and endless trouble awaited the coming of the first woman who had offered to enter the English military hospitals as a nurse?

There was but little time for preparation. All that brain and hands could do must be done in a week, but Florence went about her work quietly and calmly. There was no bustle or hurry, everything was done methodically, and only once was her calmness upset. This was when she heard of the death of her little pet owl which she had brought from Greece.

It had tumbled out of its nest in the Parthenon and Florence had rescued it and brought it safely home, it having travelled mostly in her pocket until they reached Embley. Now, in the hurry and bustle, the owl had been forgotten and it had died of starvation.

"The only tear its mistress shed through that tremendous week," says her sister, "was when I put the little body into her hands. 'Poor little beastie, it was odd how much I loved you,' she said sadly."

Perhaps the most difficult part of the work was the choosing of the nurses, for this had to be done most carefully. They were to be not merely good women but women who had had some training and would be fit for the work. Some of them were taken from a Roman Catholic sisterhood, some were Anglican sisters, and others from different English hospitals. Scarcely any were of gentle birth, but they all had had some experience of nursing.

The night before they started, all the nurses, thirty-eight in number, were gathered in Mr. Herbert's dining-room, and he warned them that now was the time to turn back if any of their hearts were failing them, but if they were ready to go forward,

HE WARNED THEM THAT NOW WAS THE TIME TO TURN
BACK IF ANY OF THEIR HEARTS WERE FALLING.

they must loyally bind themselves to obey Miss Nightingale in all things.

So the brave little band started out and arrived at the barrack hospital at Scutari, not long after the Battle of Balaclava had been fought, and on the very day of the Battle of Inkerman.

It is true that the nurses had expected to find things in a very bad state, but the reality was far worse than anyone had dreamed of. Not only were the wards frightfully overcrowded, but they were terribly dirty and the air was horrible to breathe. There were not enough beds to go round, and the canvas sheets were so coarse that the men begged to be left in their blankets. There was no furniture of any kind, and only beer or wine bottles for candlesticks. Medical and surgical appliances were lacking, the food was impossible, and the whole place was overrun with rats.

All during the voyage out, Florence had been thinking and planning what should be done on their arrival, and when one of the nurses told her that she hoped there would be no delays but that they would begin at once to nurse the poor fellows, she answered calmly, "The strongest will be wanted at the wash-tub." But even she had not expected quite such a want of cleanliness. Not a basin nor a towel nor a piece of soap was to be found! The men's shirts had never been washed, nor their sheets either. Three hundred scrubbing brushes and two hundred hard scrubbers was the first thing Miss Nightingale demanded, and then she took a Turkish house and had boilers put into it, and employed the soldiers' wives to do the washing, and in a short time there were, at least, clean floors and clean beds in the hospital wards.

The next thing to be done was to provide proper food, and so extra kitchens were soon established and dainty nourishment prepared for the patients. All this was paid for partly out of Miss Nightingale's own purse and partly out of the money subscribed at home. There was no difficulty too great for the Lady-in-Chief to grapple with and none that she did not overcome. One of the wounded soldiers remembered her passing his bed with some of the doctors who were saying, "It can't be done," and he never forgot the great determination of her voice as she answered, "It **MUST** be done."

She seldom spared others, but then she never spared herself. Everything was referred to her, and there never seemed time for rest. One of her friends, Miss Stanley, wrote home an interesting account of post day at the hospital, when the Lady-in-Chief sat behind her screen in the kitchen, trying to write her dispatches: "A stream of people every minute.

'Please, ma'am, have you any black-edged paper?' 'Please, what can I give which would keep on his stomach? Is there any arrowroot today for him?' 'No; the tubs of arrowroot must be for the worst cases; we cannot spare him any, nor is there any jelly today; try him with some eggs.' 'Please, Mr. Gordon, the Chief Engineer, wishes to see Miss Nightingale about the orders she gave him.' Mr. Sabin comes in for something else. Mr. Bracebridge in and out about General Adams and orders of various kinds."

Calm in the midst of worry and bustle, the Lady-in-Chief did her work and gave all directions. It was not only kindness of heart that made her help so valuable; it was her clear head, her judgment, her experience, and knowledge. She herself required much more of her nurses than goodness of heart and a love of nursing, and in one of her notes she mentions how little use she had for "excellent, gentle, self-devoted women, fit more for Heaven than a hospital. They flit about like angels without hands among the patients and soothe their souls, while they leave their bodies dirty and neglected." It was pleasant to have her nurses real ministering angels, but the Lady-in-Chief insisted on hands as well as haloes.

Now there were quite a number of people who objected most strongly to the coming of Miss Nightingale and her nurses, and this helped to make their work most difficult. From Lord Raglan she received nothing but kindness and consideration, but there were many doctors and officers who resented this new arrangement. Such a thing as women nurses had never before been known in the British army, and they were both angry and jealous at the idea of this "meddling."

It was a difficult time indeed for the head nurse. Here were shiploads of wounded soldiers arriving, no beds to put them on, no proper food or clothing ready for them, tiresome under-nurses to be trained, jealous people in authority to be pacified, reports to be sent to the home government, and four miles of beds to be looked after. It would seem to need someone with a magic wand to do all that was required. Yet it was all done — and all well done too — and the magic was one woman's marvellous brain, willing hands, and great heart.

There seemed something almost uncanny about Florence Nightingale's power and influence. She made people do as she wanted even against their will. She managed to get her own way in a manner which fell little short of magic. The soldiers, of course, adored her. They fully believed she could do anything, even to the working of miracles. Just to look at her as she passed and to touch the hem of her garment put fresh heart into them. As one poor fellow wrote home, "What a comfort it was to see her pass even. She would speak to one and nod and smile to as many more; but she could not do it to all, you know. We lay there by hundreds; but we could kiss her shadow as it fell, and lay our heads on the pillow again, content." Another one wrote, "Before she came there was cussin' and swearin', but after that it was holy as a church."

When night came on and all was dark and silent in the wards, the slender figure in its red cape and grey gown went noiselessly from bed to bed, carrying in her hand a little lamp which shone like a star of hope in that abode of pain. Eyes full of adoring gratitude watched her pass, rough soldiers turned

EYES FALL OF ADORING GRATITUDE WATCHED HER PASS.

and kissed her shadow as it fell upon their pillows. The stern head nurse, with her strict rules and regulations—the woman who planned and carried out vast reforms, the Lady-in-Chief who stood her ground with the highest officials—was to those poor men their "Lady of the Lamp," their ministering angel, whose wings were only folded and hidden away out of sight.

"If the soldiers were told that the roof had opened and she had gone up palpably to Heaven, they would not have been in the least surprised," said one of her friends who had gone out to help Miss Nightingale. "If the Queen came for to die," said one of the wounded soldiers, "they ought to make her queen, and I think they would."

In the "dreaded room" where operations were performed, the presence of their dear and honoured Lady-in-Chief made these poor soldiers strong to suffer. When she stood at their side "with lips closely set and hands folded, decreeing herself to go through the pain of witnessing pain," the very sight of her gave them a strange kind of strength and made them ready to endure. She had no thought for herself; her only desire was to help and to give out of her large heart all the sympathy and comfort and support which the poor men looked for.

The overworked doctors were obliged to set aside the hopeless cases when the men were carried in and attend first to those which had a better chance of recovery, but the hopeless cases were the special charge of the Lady-in-Chief. Nursing and good food sometimes worked wonders, and we know of one instance when five soldiers, set aside as hopeless by the surgeons, were carefully nursed all night by Miss Nightingale and some of her nurses, and by the next morning were found to be quite fit to undergo surgical treatment.

"I believe," wrote one of the doctors who worked with her, "that there was never a severe case of any kind that escaped her notice, and sometimes it was wonderful to see her at the bedside of a patient, who had been admitted perhaps but an hour before, and of whose arrival one would hardly have supposed it possible she could be already cognisant."

Even at the time it must have cheered her greatly to see the daily and hourly results of all she was

FIVE SOLDIERS, SET ASIDE AS HOPELESS BY THE SURGEONS, WERE CAREFULLY
NURSED ALL NIGHT BY MISS NIGHTINGALE AND SOME OF HER NURSES.

doing, but could she have looked into the future
and seen the Red Cross Societies throughout all
the world, which were to be the fruit of that seed
she was sowing, it would have made it even more
worth while.

It was not only for the soldiers themselves that
she stood as a tower of strength and consolation.
Many a wife and mother in England blessed her for

POST DAY AT THE HOSPITAL, WHEN THE LADY-IN-CHIEF SAT BEHIND
HER SCREEN IN THE KITCHEN, TRYING TO WRITE HER DESPATCHES.

her wonderful goodness and consideration. She was never too busy to send letters and messages home; no one appealed to her in vain for news of the soldiers under her care, and so it was that from English homes, as well as from the foreign hospitals, there arose from thousands of hearts that one prayer, "God bless her."

It is good to remember too that if the soldiers looked upon her as a saint, their saint in return had a splendid tribute to pay to them, as she declared afterwards: "Tears come into my eyes as I think how amidst scenes of loathsome disease and death, there arose above it all the innate dignity, gentleness and chivalry of the men, shining in the midst of what must be considered as the lowest sinks of human misery, and preventing instinctively the use of an expression which could distress a gentlewoman."

CHAPTER IV

FAITHFUL TO THE END

AFTER that terrible winter of the siege of Sebastopol, the hospital at Scutari was less crowded, and in such good working order that the Lady-in-Chief made up her mind to go to the Crimea and inspect the hospitals there.

These hospitals were already supplied with nurses and superintendents, but they were all responsible to Miss Nightingale, and she wished to see for herself how the work was being done.

That visit to the front was something which Florence Nightingale never forgot. Wherever she went, she was received with enthusiasm, and cheers rang out from the soldiers as they watched her ride past to call on Lord Raglan. It was a greeting which touched her heart, for she felt it a great honour to be cheered by those men who had fought and suffered like heroes.

She was never tired of telling tales of the heroism of those Crimean soldiers — how they lay in the trenches sometimes as long as forty-eight hours in the bitter cold, their only food raw salt pork sprinkled with sugar, rum, and biscuit — and yet how they kept up their courage and enthusiasm and eagerness to fight.

"When I see the camp," she wrote home, "I wonder not that the army has suffered so much, but that there is any army left at all." She goes on to tell of a sergeant on picket duty who, when all the rest of the picket were killed, tried to stumble back to the camp, badly wounded as he was. On the way, he came across another wounded man and somehow managed to carry him on his shoulders as far as the lines, where he fell down senseless. When he came to himself in hospital, he eagerly asked after his wounded comrade.

"Is he alive?" he asked.

"He's alive, right enough," was the answer, "but you needn't call him comrade. Why, it was the General himself."

Just then the General came to the bedside, scarcely able to walk, but anxious to thank the brave man who had saved his life.

"Oh, General," said the sergeant, "it's you, is it, that I brought in. I'm so glad. I didn't know your honour, but if I'd known it was you, I'd have saved you all the same."

"This is the true soldier's spirit," added Florence Nightingale.

There was a great deal to be done in the Crimean hospitals, and as usual the Lady-in-Chief did not spare herself. She was never the least afraid of infection, and she nursed the fever patients just as she had done at Scutari. But work and worry had at last told upon her health, and one night she complained of being "very tired," and next day the news spread far and near that Miss Nightingale was stricken with Crimean fever.

She was carried on a stretcher by relays of soldiers to the Castle Hospital, high up on the hillside, and there in a hut amongst the wounded soldiers, she fought a hard fight with death and came off conqueror.

There was terrible anxiety both at home and among the soldiers when it was known how near death she lay. Queen Victoria asked that bulletins should be sent to her as soon as they arrived, and when at last it was announced that the danger was past, she and all her people rejoiced together.

From the very first, Queen Victoria had taken the greatest interest in Florence Nightingale and realized how much the country owed to her. "I wish we had her at the War Office," she said on one occasion, when a clear head and sound judgment was specially needed.

She was anxious to see the letters which Miss Nightingale sent home, that she might have news of the wounded soldiers, and it was through the Lady-in-Chief that she sent all kinds of comforts which she thought might be useful in hospital.

"I wish Miss Nightingale and the ladies would tell those poor noble wounded and sick men," wrote the Queen, "that *no one* takes a warmer interest or feels more for their sufferings or admires their courage and heroism more than their Queen. Day and night she thinks of her beloved troops." It was a message which made the soldiers' eyes shine with pride and devotion.

"To think of her thinking of us," said one. "I only wish I could go and fight for her again."

Now once more came another royal message, this time a thanksgiving for the life of the brave woman who had come so near to laying it down for the sake of Her Majesty's soldiers.

There were rejoicings in the little hut on the Genoese heights, but the patient was still very weak and needed great care. When at last she was able to be moved, she went in a yacht to Scutari, and a barge, such as was used to remove the sick and wounded, was brought alongside and Miss Nightingale was lowered into it. A large crowd had gathered at the pier to welcome her, and there was not a more touching sight in all the campaign than the eager throng which followed the little procession as the four guardsmen carried along the litter in which their Lady-in-Chief lay.

As soon as it was known that Miss Nightingale was recovering and was determined to go back to her work and to stay at her post until the war was ended, a great wave of enthusiasm swept over England. A great desire arose to give her some per-

THE FOUR GUARDSMEN CARRIED ALONG THE LITTER IN WHICH THEIR
LADY-IN-CHIEF LAY.

sonal token of the love and admiration which filled all hearts to overflowing. A great meeting was held to consider what was to be done, and that meeting alone was a great tribute to the Lady-in-Chief. For herself, however, she would accept nothing, and finally it was decided to start a "Nightingale Fund" to help her to found a training home for nurses when the war should be over.

But this was not enough for Queen Victoria. She wanted Miss Nightingale to have some special mark of royal gratitude and appreciation, and there arrived ere long a splendid brooch or badge, designed by Prince Consort. It was in the form of a St. George's Cross, in red enamel, with the royal monogram above and a crown of diamonds. Round the badge were inscribed the words, "Blessed are the merciful," and the word "Crimea," while on the back was engraved, "To Miss Florence Nightingale, as a mark of esteem and gratitude for her devotion towards the Queen's brave soldiers. — From Victoria R. 1855."

Perhaps Florence Nightingale valued even more the letter which came with the gift, but the Queen's brooch was the pride and delight of the soldiers' hearts. Nothing was too great an honour for their beloved Lady-in-Chief. She might indeed have stood for a second Joan of Arc, so great was her power over the men, while on the other hand there were not a few officials who would have been quite ready to burn her at the stake!

The weary war dragged on, and now the Lady-in-

Chief was back at her post. There were many who thought she ought to go home after her illness, but she could not be persuaded to leave the sick and wounded soldiers who needed her care.

"Whatever should we do without her?" asked the men; and they added, "We all set our hopes on Her."

Indeed, there were not a few who firmly believed that if she were at their head, they would be in Sebastopol in a week!

"I am ready to stand out the war with any man," said Florence Nightingale, and she more than proved her words, for even after the fall of Sebastopol, when peace was declared, she worked on for nearly a year in the Crimea and at Scutari. It was perhaps the hardest work of all then, for the hospitals were far apart and the roads between were terribly bad, so that in winter the travelling was most dangerous. At first, she drove in a cart drawn by a mule, but afterwards the Commandant of the Transport Corps gave her a vehicle which was dignified by the name of "Miss Nightingale's carriage," but which was only a hooded baggage-car, guiltless of springs.

In this car, or on horseback if the roads were too

"Miss Nightingale's Carriage"

bad for driving, Miss Nightingale went her rounds, and no weather was bad enough to stop her. She would never spare herself, even when suffering from rheumatism and agonizing sciatica. She was always "strong to endure."

The soldiers indeed owed more to their Lady-in-Chief than they realized, for she was their good friend as well as their ministering angel. Her personal influence was so great that the men could not bear to do anything that they knew would displease her, and gradually there was less drinking, less disorder, and bad language amongst them. "I promised Her I wouldn't drink," a soldier would say, and that was reason enough for anyone.

Instead of squandering their pay, she persuaded them to send money home to their wives and families, and herself undertook all the trouble of having it done. All their affairs were of interest to her, and as they began to get better, she started reading-rooms and class-rooms for them, and so kept them busy and out of the mischief which Satan always finds for idle hands to do.

Everyone at home was eager to help with these

reading-rooms, "from the Royal Family to the humblest printer's boy," and many were the curious offerings sent out to Miss Nightingale for this work. The P. & O. Company carried all the things free of charge, and very soon there was enough material to start schools and reading-rooms both in the Crimea and at Scutari. The reading-rooms were constantly used by crowds of the convalescent

THE READING-ROOMS WERE CONSTANTLY USED BY
CROWDS OF THE CONVALESCENT SOLDIERS.

soldiers, and the Lady-in-Chief spoke proudly of their good behaviour. They were "uniformly quiet and well bred," she said, and she was more than rewarded for all her trouble.

At last, the time came when the hospitals were almost empty and the nurses had all gone and the Lady-in-Chief was free to return home. The Government offered a man-of-war to carry her back in triumph, but this she at once refused. Her one idea was to get home as quietly as she could and to escape as much public notice as possible. The whole country was ready to welcome her with addresses and triumphal arches and regimental bands, but while they anxiously awaited news of her arrival, she landed unnoticed, spent a quiet night with the nuns at Bermondsey, took an early train home to Lea Hurst the next morning, and walked up from the little country station unrecognized. "A little tinkle of the small church bell on the hills, and a thanksgiving prayer at the little chapel next day," wrote her sister, "were all the innocent greeting."

Her "spoils of war," as Parthe called them, had arrived before her. First, there was William, the one-legged sailor boy who had been ten months in her hospital; then there was Peter, a little Russian prisoner who was an orphan and therefore a special charge. Peter had been asked once by a nurse where he would go to if he was a good boy, and he answered promptly, without a shadow of doubt, "To Miss Nightingale." Besides these two, there was a big Crimean puppy, a gift from her soldiers, which had been found in a hole in the rocks near Balaclava. A little Russian cat had died on its way home, but the rest of the "spoil" were in excellent health and spirits, and, as the old fairy tales say, "lived happily ever after."

There was one other thing which Florence Nightingale brought home which perhaps was too sacred to show even to her sister. It was a bunch of withered grass, "picked out of the ground watered by our men's blood at Inkerman."

CHAPTER V

WORK AT HOME

FLORENCE NIGHTINGALE had certainly earned a rest, and rest was what she now needed above all things, but as long as there was anything she could do for the soldiers, "my children," as she called them, it seemed impossible for her to think of herself and her own needs.

She knew that thousands of those children of hers need not have died if they had been properly cared for, and the thought would not let her rest. She could not bring them back to life, but she might help to prevent others from sharing their fate. She was filled with a burning desire to reform the Army Medical Service and to make it impossible that such things should happen again.

"No one," she wrote, "can feel for the army as I do. These people who talk to us have all fed their children on the fat of the land and dressed them in velvet and silk, while we have been away. I have had to see my children dressed in a dirty blanket and an old pair of regimental trousers, and to see them fed on raw salt meat, and nine thousand of my children are lying, from causes which might have been prevented, in their forgotten graves. But I can never forget."

Not only did she feel, as no one else did, the urgent need of reform, but there was perhaps no one else so fitted to carry it out. The ministering angel of the Scutari hospital was a very human angel, the "Lady with the Lamp" carried with her the light of a wonderful intelligence, the saint was a person of very strong character and possessed a wonderful working brain. Then, too, her position was a great advantage to her, and public opinion, which she valued but lightly for her own sake, was of solid advantage to her work. Those in high places were only too glad to ask her advice and help. She was invited by the Queen to Balmoral and the visit was a great success. Very plainly she told the tale of what had happened in the hospitals and very clearly she pointed out how much there now remained to be done.

"Such a clear head," exclaimed the Queen. "I wish we had her at the War Office."

It is impossible here to follow her through her work for "the Salvation of the British Army." With Mr. Herbert, afterwards Lord Herbert of Lea, to help her, she carried out her scheme of hospital reform in a way that seems little short of magic when we realize that she was an invalid, frail and suffering, "only a woman," who yet could influence and direct the cleverest men in the country. The difficulties in her path were tremendous, and she had to fight against old-fashioned prejudice and obstinacy, but the "Nightingale power" which had worked such wonders in the Crimea was as strong a force as ever and made itself felt all through her work.

There was no detail too small to escape her notice, no problem too great for her mind to grasp. Her body might suffer but her spirit was always equal to the task. To watch her at work was, as someone described it, like "watching a gigantic game of chess, whereof the pawns were men and the result the lives of thousands."

To do this work Florence Nightingale gave up

everything else. Even her own family saw but little of her. She was scarcely ever at Embley or Lea Hurst now, but took up her abode in London, in the Burlington Hotel, where her room came to be known as "the little War Office." There she saw only her "Cabinet" of reformers and held her councils. Great politicians and famous men came to that room for help and advice. She used to say she had no drawing-room, "a thing which is the destruction of so many women's lives," but the council chamber was almost always made beautiful by the flowers she loved, and there was often a cat to be seen there too, for she loved animals as much as ever. "There are always flowers in her rooms," wrote a cousin, "but so many Blue-books that I should think she could not complain of their looking like drawing-rooms."

There was much work to be done, and the invalid had so little strength to spare that her friends began to be seriously afraid that the strain would prove too great for her. "She is killing herself with work (which they all say no one else can do, no one else has the threads of it, or the perseverance for it), and yet no one will ever know it. Others will have all the credit of the very things she suggested and introduced, at the cost, one may say, of life and comfort of all kinds, for it is an intolerable life she is leading — lying down between whiles to enable her just to go on, not seeing her nearest and dearest, because, with her breath so hurried, all talking must be spared except what is necessary, and all excitement that she may devote every energy to the work."

Few guessed that the great reforms carried out in the Army Medical Service were due principally to Florence Nightingale. Her name stood, indeed, for a saint, a ministering angel whose work was now done and who lived the life of a suffering invalid, but England could not know what that invalid was doing still for her soldiers. The real Florence Nightingale was much greater than the gentle saint whom the British public pictured so reverently. The work she had done during the war, in the hospitals, was a noble work indeed, but what she was doing now was even greater.

It was a work that could not be done in a hurry, but by and by the soldiers' barracks were gradually remodelled and made healthy, a school of cookery was established, the Army Medical School was founded, and the soldiers were cared for when in health as well as when sickness came. Reading-rooms, coffee-rooms and lecture-rooms were started, and, indeed, both Mr. Herbert and the invalid lady well deserved their name of "the soldiers' friend."

But it was not only the health of the soldiers for which Florence Nightingale worked. It was not only the military hospitals which needed to be reformed. The whole art of nursing both in public hospitals and private homes was in a very bad way, and the invalid could not rest until she had set to work to improve matters.

Florence Nightingale was more of a worker than a writer but when she did use her pen it was always to some purpose. Now, her "Notes on Nursing" sounded like a trumpet-call to the country and directed public attention to the reforms she demanded. She drew out plans of hospitals which were, ere long, built. She arranged about the training of nurses, and made out rules and regulations. It has been well said that there were three famous persons in the nineteenth century to whom the country owed supreme gratitude for what they had done to relieve human suffering, and these were Simpson, who introduced chloroform, Lister, who invented antiseptic surgery, and Florence Nightingale, who was the founder of modern nursing.

Now, although Florence Nightingale took but little pleasure in her own popularity, it helped most enormously in this great work of hers. Her very name inspired trust and enthusiasm. The whole nation had been thrilled by the account of what she had done and suffered for the soldiers in the Crimean War. Not only in high places but in the humblest cottage her name was known and held in reverence. Little children lisped her name in a kind of belief that she was a fairy queen or guardian angel, and to young girls she was an inspiration. Her example broke down the barriers which generations had built up around young ladyhood. As she herself, in her youth, had fought for freedom, so now she made it possible for others to be free.

Thus it was, that when the invalid lady called for

women to help her to raise the standard of nursing in this country, there were hundreds all ready, fired by her example, to answer the call.

"Notes on Nursing" was perhaps one of the best of the books she wrote. "It is so real and so intense, that it will, I doubt not, create an Order of Nurses before it has finished its work," wrote Harriet Martineau.

The book was read by all sorts and conditions of people, both at home and abroad. It had as much to do with the care of the home as the nursing in hospitals. It would be as useful today to anyone who really cared to learn how to be a helpful nurse at home. The very fact that it was written by one who had learned by experience all that she now tried to teach made it a living thing. It was by no means a book of mere thoughts about nursing; it was written to show people what to *do*. So practical was the author that, by and by, she added some notes on "Minding Baby" to help even little schoolgirls take their share in her work.

But Florence Nightingale did more for the cause than setting an example and giving good advice. She set to work herself to do something.

The "Nightingale Fund," which had been the Nation's personal gift to her, she now decided to use for the training of hospital nurses, two-thirds of it to be spent on her own special Nightingale nurses who were to be trained at S. Thomas' Hospital. Later on, when the hospital was rebuilt, the Nightingale Training Home became a part of that great building on the Thames Embankment.

Everything about this home was done under the direction of the invalid; each minutest detail was planned by her. She interviewed all the probationers and took a personal interest in each one of them, even making notes of their characters. The school started with only fifteen probationers, and of these, thirteen finished their training and were ready to go out and spread the good work. It seemed a small beginning and but a tiny field in which to sow the seed, but the harvest today shows upon what good ground it was sown.

All this time, it must be remembered, Florence Nightingale was hard at work with Mr. Herbert in the Army Medical Reform as well. She had even offered, in spite of ill-health, to go out to India at the time of the Indian Mutiny. She always looked upon herself as a soldier and, like a soldier, was always keen on active service, although she was serving so well at home.

The death of Lord Herbert came as a great blow to the brave lady. He had been her helper through the Crimean War, her ally in the fight at home, her constant companion and fellow-worker for five busy years. It was not only personally that she grieved for him, but she thought that his death would bring her work to a standstill, and she cared more for her work than life itself.

For a while, the loss of her "dear master" seemed to overwhelm her, but at length, she was roused to try and carry on the work which he had left unfinished. It was before Lord Herbert's death that she had begun to make her plans for the improvement of the health of our soldiers in India. Like everything else she took in hand, she did this most thoroughly, and the knowledge she acquired of India and Indian subjects was so great that it was difficult to believe she had never been in that country.

Ill and lonely, for she had now lost her much-loved cousin Arthur Clough as well as her "dear master," she toiled on with the great work. She made friends of ministers who were likely to be of use, and she used all her wonderful power to the uttermost.

It was her dearest wish when Lord Elgin died that Sir John Lawrence should be made Viceroy of India. Not only was he a soldier after her own heart, not only had she been thrilled by his heroic deeds and felt sure that he was the strong man needed to command in India, but he was almost as keen as she was on the question of sanitary reform. If he was at the head of affairs, she felt sure her work would be carried through.

No one knew better than Florence Nightingale when and where to speak a word in due season, and her word carried more weight than the outside world guessed. To her great joy, in the end, her wish was granted, and she had an interview with the new Viceroy which she never forgot. He called to see her before he left for his post, although he had only ten days before starting, and together the famous soldier and the frail invalid discussed grave questions of national importance and made their plans, which were to work a reformation in India.

It was not only for council but for inspiration that so many great men went to that "little War Office," and they never failed to carry away a sense of the power which lay in that marvelous brain. Sir John Lawrence often wrote afterward to report progress, and it was said in after years that "men used to say they always knew when the Viceroy had received a letter from Florence Nightingale; it was like the ringing of a bell to call for sanitary progress."

Now that it has been permitted to look over her private papers, it is extraordinary to see the influence she must have exerted. The letters she received from ministers show that every vexed question at the War Office (except those of a purely military kind) was referred to her. She was the expert whose opinion was always considered worth attention.

There is a large volume written telling of all she did both at home and abroad, the splendid reforms she helped to carry out in India, the help she gave in the Franco-German war, the fight with the work-house infirmaries in which she came out trium-

TOGETHER THE FAMOUS SOLDIER AND THE FRAIL INVALID
DISCUSSED GRAVE QUESTIONS OF NATIONAL IMPORTANCE.

phant. As long as she was able, she worked, and
then came the time when she could do no more,
when the dust and heat of the working day was
over, when the evening shadows began to fall and
she waited for the quiet night of rest.

CHAPTER VI

EVENTIDE

IN those twilight hours, we still catch glimpses of the "Lady with the Lamp." We see her "propped up in bed, the pillows framing her kindly face with its lace-covered silvery hair," bidding God-speed to one of her nurses about to leave for service in the Soudan. The nurse describes the practical kindliness of that good-bye, the delicious breakfast of coffee, toast, eggs, and honey. "A real English breakfast, dear child," she said, "and it is good to know you will have honestly earned the next one you eat in England." "And suppose I don't return to eat one at all?" I asked. "Well, you will have earned that too, dear heart," she answered quietly. "Who can be surprised that we worshipped our Chief?"

We see her, too, listening with liveliest interest to anything connected with the work in India, and as anxious as ever to fight the battle for her nurses at home.

"Am I not tiring you?" asked a nurse, as she told of work and patients and plans for improvements.

"Oh, no," answered Miss Nightingale quickly, "you give me new life."

Perhaps she scarcely understood the honour she received when King Edward presented her with the Order of Merit. She was so near the Master whom she had so faithfully served that earth's voices sounded but dimly in her ears, and she had always rather dreaded the world's praise.

"Too kind, too kind," was all she said.

There was only one thing now that could bring the old light into her eye and fix her wandering attention. Even talk about nursing failed to interest her, but the very mention of soldiers was like a trumpet-call which her ears were never too dull to hear and to which her mind answered to the end.

Rest came at last. She who had so bravely fought the good fight had now finished her labours. She passed away peacefully, as she slept, on a summer afternoon on the 13th of August 1910, resting quietly after her ninety years of life.

She had left directions that her funeral should

be as simple as possible, so it was decided that she should be buried in the churchyard near her own home, and not in Westminster Abbey. Six of her soldier "children," sergeants, taken from the several regiments of the Guards, had the honour of carrying her body to its last resting-place, and although the funeral was kept as private as possible, the way was lined with a great crowd of people — men, women, and children, mostly poor folk — who were sorrowing as if for a personal friend.

So the "Lady of the Lamp" passed on, but the light of the burning torch she kindled can never die, and many an inspiration will be kindled at its flame, many a one urged by her example to "follow the gleam" which leads to all that is highest and best.

> "On England's annals, through the long
> Hereafter of her speech and song,
> That light its rays shall cast
> From portals of the past.
>
> A Lady with a Lamp shall stand
> In the great history of the land,
> A noble type of good
> Heroic womanhood."

www.ingramcontent.com/pod-product-compliance
Lightning Source LLC
Chambersburg PA
CBHW032022180726
48283CB00008B/2801